KSD Cenyp

ACB 3595

SANTA CRUZ CITY-COUNTY LIBRARY SYSTEM

D0520665

JEASY

Willard, Nancy.

The sorcerer's
apprentice /
1993.

8/95

DISCARD

10/97 ⑩

SANTA CRUZ PUBLIC LIBRARY

SANTA CRUZ, CALIFORNIA 95060

The Sorcerer's Apprentice

BY NANCY WILLARD

ILLUSTRATED BY LEO AND DIANE DILLON

THE BLUE SKY PRESS

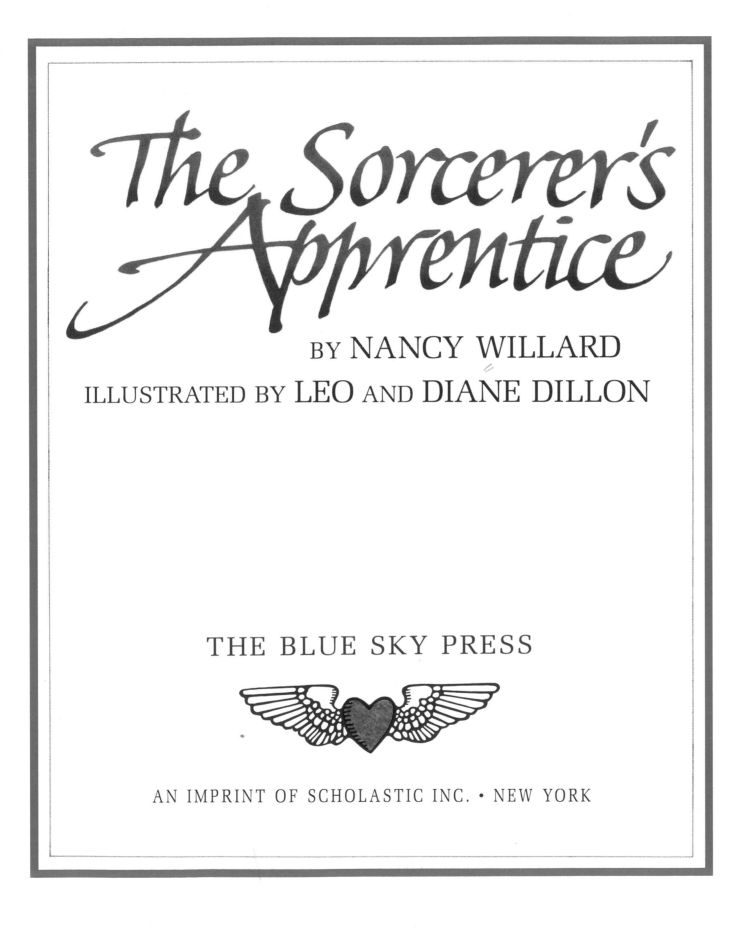

AN IMPRINT OF SCHOLASTIC INC. • NEW YORK

SANTA CRUZ PUBLIC LIBRARY
Santa Cruz, California

The Blue Sky Press

●

Text copyright © 1993 by Nancy Willard
Illustrations copyright © 1993 by Leo Dillon and Diane Dillon
All rights reserved.
No part of this publication may be reproduced
or stored in a retrieval system
or transmitted in any form or by any means,
electronic, mechanical, photocopying, recording,
or otherwise, without written permission
of the publisher.
For information regarding permission,
please write to:
Permissions Department,
The Blue Sky Press,
an imprint of Scholastic Inc.,
555 Broadway, New York, New York 10012
The Blue Sky Press is a trademark of Scholastic Inc.

Library of Congress Cataloging-in-Publication Data
Willard, Nancy.
The sorcerer's apprentice / Nancy Willard; illustrated by
Leo and Diane Dillon.
p. cm.
Summary: Sylvia, the new apprentice to the great magician Tottibo,
steals one of his spells to complete an impossible task and
accidentally creates chaos.
ISBN 0-590-47329-8
[1. Magicians — Fiction. 2. Magic — Fiction.] I. Dillon, Leo,
ill. II. Dillon, Diane, ill. III. Dillon, Leo, ill. IV. Title.
PZ7.W6553So 1993
[E] — dc20   93-19912
CIP
AC
12 11 10 9 8 7 6 5 4 3 2 1   3 4 5 6 7 8/9
Printed in the United States of America   36
First printing, October 19, 1993

●

The full-page illustrations in this book were executed in watercolors
on Arches hot press watercolor paper mounted on board,
and the spot illustrations were executed in watercolors
on Strathmore three-ply kid-finish bristol board.
The full-page illustrations were spot-varnished, and the book was printed on 100-pound
Karma Cream paper, using a fifth-color gold ink throughout for the borders.
The geometric symbol worn by the sorcerer in this book was devised by the artists
because of its meaning: the triangle stands for creative intellect,
and the circle represents eternity — combined,
they signify endless creativity.
The display type was hand-lettered by Jeanyee Wong.
The text type was set in Melior Condensed by Characters Graphic Services, New York, New York.
Color separations were made by Color Dot Graphics, Inc., St. Louis, Missouri.
Printed and bound by Horowitz/Rae Book Manufacturers, Inc., Fairfield, New Jersey
Production supervision by Angela Biola
Art direction by Claire Counihan
Designed by Leo and Diane Dillon

For Bonnie
—N.W.

For Bonnie, Nancy, Claire,
Elizabeth, and Lee
—L. & D.D.

Mount Dragon's Eyes? It's very near,
yet no one travels it for fear
of beasts that mutter, huff, and blow,
round the magician Tottibo.
Beyond his house the earth looks dead.
"Take heart, you beasts and bugs," he said.
"Let spiders sing and panthers play.
My new apprentice comes today!"

Her bike was blue, her hair was red.
The road turned wicked, sharp, and sly.
The footpath ended in a sigh.
Sylvia dismounted, combed her hair,
took a deep breath and climbed the stair.

The house had fifty-seven doors
that snapped and growled
and groaned and roared,
and knockers made of gnashing teeth,
which mercifully hung out of reach.
A rusty ax hung in the air.
She wondered who had put it there.
The house had ninety-seven eyes—
    cats' eyes, bats' eyes,
    snake eyes, fake eyes,
    and bottom-of-the-lake eyes.

Two spiders left their leafy looms.
A gryphon cocked his bitten ear.
The panther beat his battered drum
and shouted, "Sylvia has come."
From twilight depths of distant rooms
a dozen mice sang, "Bring her here."

On a high stool with silver feet,
a ring of dragons round his seat,
a one-eyed cat, a singing cane
that flexed and scratched its ruby toe,
and other beasts without a name,
sat their fierce master Tottibo
with book and bottle high in hand,
and though the glass held only sand,
it shrugged and coiled,
reeked and roiled,
sparked and spankled, beeped and boiled.

Sylvia bowed, a little nervous.
"Your new apprentice, at your service."
The old magician stood so tall
his very shadow chilled them all
as he delivered his command.

"Your first task is to make new clothes
for all the creatures in my care—
new caps, new capes, new vests and hose.
I need a dozen bibs well matched,
for baby dragons newly hatched,
gauntlets for gryphons young and bold
whose taste inclines to cloth of gold,
windbreakers for a dozen wings,
and cloaks to clothe the lesser things
my magic calls from caves as deep
as breath of stars or dragon's sleep.
For plump or puny, large or lean,
you'll have my trusty sewing machine."

"But I want magic," Sylvia cried,
"bottles and jars of magic stuff.
You have a ruby-footed cane.
I want a diamond in the rough
and spells to make it bright again."

Tottibo frowned at her and sighed.
"You must take special care with potions,
syrups and essences and lotions.
You know the work will not go well
if you should mispronounce a spell.
A single lapse in common sense
can have a fatal consequence.
The last apprentice took no time
to learn a complicated rhyme
that turned a lily to a lock.
He turned into a hollyhock.
For magic free of aggravation,
practice. And now, a demonstration."

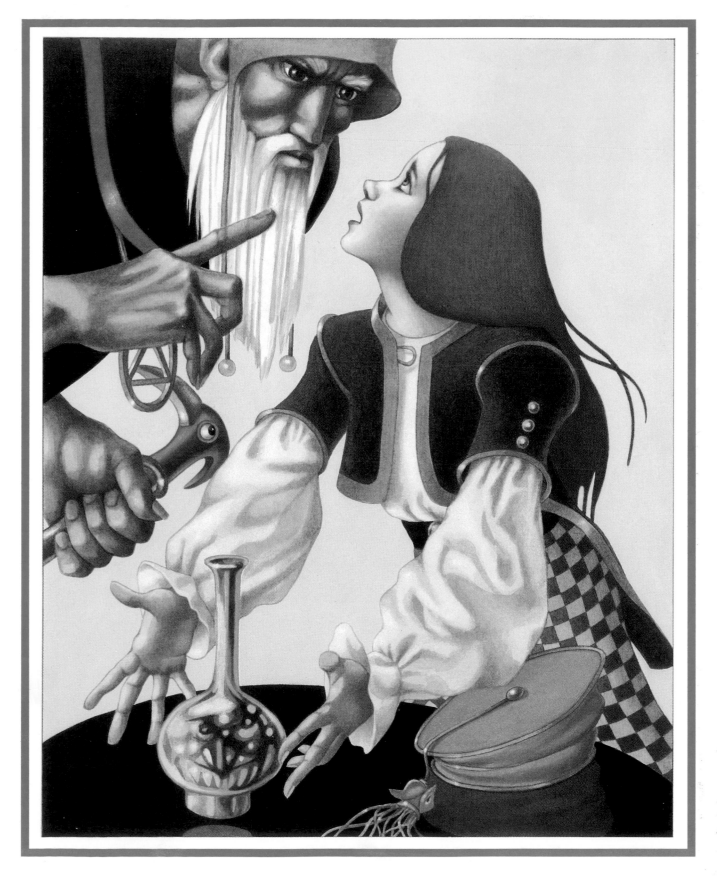

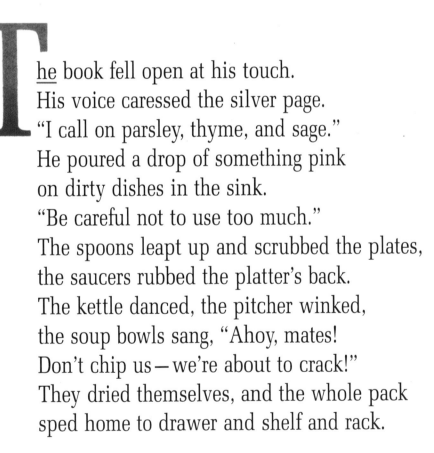

The book fell open at his touch.
His voice caressed the silver page.
"I call on parsley, thyme, and sage."
He poured a drop of something pink
on dirty dishes in the sink.
"Be careful not to use too much."
The spoons leapt up and scrubbed the plates,
the saucers rubbed the platter's back.
The kettle danced, the pitcher winked,
the soup bowls sang, "Ahoy, mates!
Don't chip us—we're about to crack!"
They dried themselves, and the whole pack
sped home to drawer and shelf and rack.

"Enough!" he cried. "The lesson's done.
Dragons and gryphons, fall in line
for thread and fabric, shears, and pins."
Sylvia bowed, and one by one
she took the measure of each tail,
each paw, each claw, each sparkling spine,
and fifty nifty flashing fins.

She cut twelve silken bibs, all matched,
for baby dragons newly hatched,
who let her chuck their scaly chins.
Gauntlets for gryphons, young and bold—
she cut them large, from cloth of gold.
Capes for the ruby-footed cane,
the drumming panther, dreaming spiders,
and half a dozen water striders,
windbreakers with a gorgeous sheen—
she cut them from blue velveteen.

By dinnertime her fingers ached,
and Sylvia was close to tears.
"I'm hungrier than fifty bears!"
Tottibo conjured up a tray
loaded with noodles, Bartlett pears,
sticky buns, muffins freshly baked,
gravy and meatloaf, lemon pie.
    "May your great appetite be curbed.
    It's time for my enchanted nap.
    I do not wish to be disturbed
    till you complete the task I set.
    Good night, good night.
    And don't forget
    to douse the light."

She cut herself a piece of pie.
The dragons leaped into her lap,
the panther heaved a hungry sigh.
The wings alit in dusky flocks
on baskets heaped with dirty socks.
The ruby-footed cane drew near,
the water striders lost their fear.
Such yapping, lapping, slurping, blurping—
"I'll never finish all these clothes!"

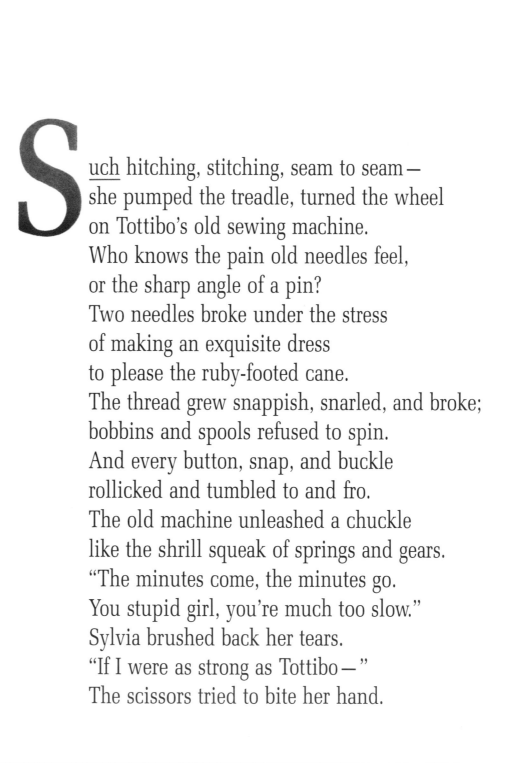

Such hitching, stitching, seam to seam—
she pumped the treadle, turned the wheel
on Tottibo's old sewing machine.
Who knows the pain old needles feel,
or the sharp angle of a pin?
Two needles broke under the stress
of making an exquisite dress
to please the ruby-footed cane.
The thread grew snappish, snarled, and broke;
bobbins and spools refused to spin.
And every button, snap, and buckle
rollicked and tumbled to and fro.
The old machine unleashed a chuckle
like the shrill squeak of springs and gears.
"The minutes come, the minutes go.
You stupid girl, you're much too slow."
Sylvia brushed back her tears.
"If I were as strong as Tottibo—"
The scissors tried to bite her hand.

A nd then she spied, on a high shelf
(under *A Guide to Weeping Wells*),
the modest bottle full of sand
beside the silver book of spells.
"For sewing free of aggravation,
I'll take some magic for myself.
One drop. And now, a demonstration."

The sand turned red, the sand turned green.
She poured it on the old machine.
Her voice caressed the silver page.
"I call on parsley, thyme, and sage."
It cleared its throat; its cogs felt sore.
She offered it a little more.
Halfway between
a smile, a frown,
its needles wheezed,
its bobbins sneezed.
She shook the bottle upside down.

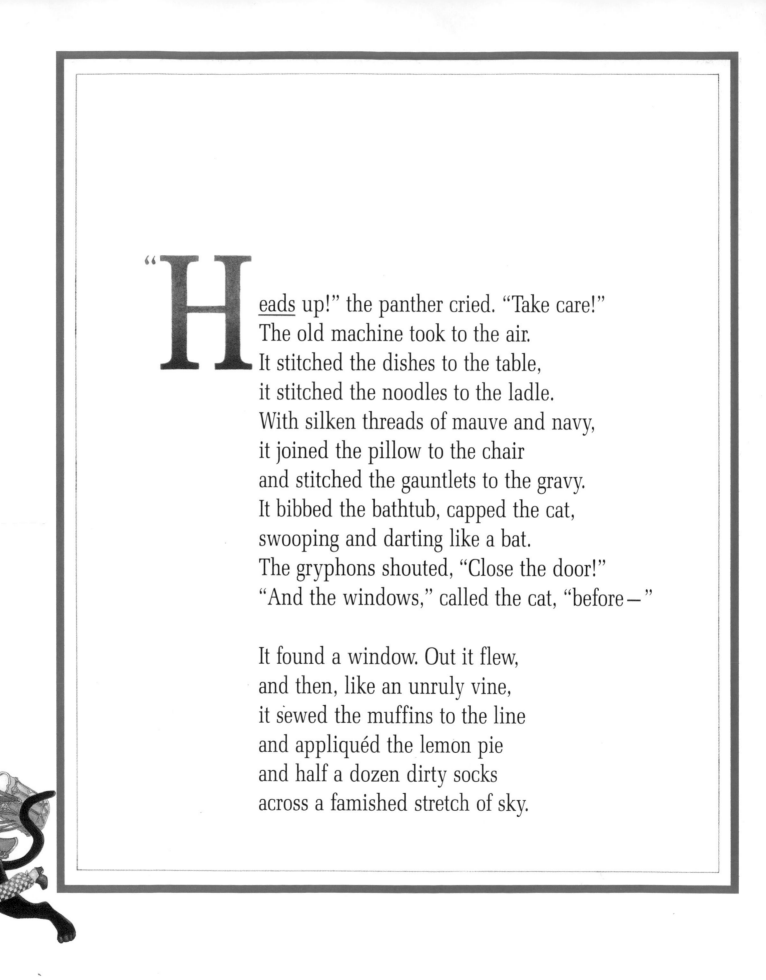

"Heads up!" the panther cried. "Take care!"
The old machine took to the air.
It stitched the dishes to the table,
it stitched the noodles to the ladle.
With silken threads of mauve and navy,
it joined the pillow to the chair
and stitched the gauntlets to the gravy.
It bibbed the bathtub, capped the cat,
swooping and darting like a bat.
The gryphons shouted, "Close the door!"
"And the windows," called the cat, "before—"

It found a window. Out it flew,
and then, like an unruly vine,
it sewed the muffins to the line
and appliquéd the lemon pie
and half a dozen dirty socks
across a famished stretch of sky.

Sylvia seized the rusty ax
and gave it four and twenty whacks.
The metal sparkled pink and green
and broke apart,
and from its heart
sprang four and twenty new machines
that cheeped and chattered,
squeaked and scattered,
snipped the moon and bit the sun
as if it were a sticky bun,
hemmed all the trees, then spun around
and stitched the mountain upside down.

Tottibo woke to fearful cries
and scarcely could believe his eyes.

He drew three circles in the sand
and wrote in letters pink and green:

"I the Great Tottibo command
all disobedient machines
be as you were before,
be one,
and let this magic spell restore
the trees, the mountain, moon and sun."

He turned to Sylvia with a sneer,
his tone and manner most severe.
"We, who are masters of these arts,
learn by our failures, fits, and starts.
If you would learn to cast a spell,
practice until you do it well."

Mount Dragon's Eyes? It's very near,
and every day not far from here,
round a high stool with silver feet,
those who would study magic meet
at Tottibo's: the one-eyed cat,
the drumming panther, singing cane,
the mice, a dozen dreamy spiders,
and half a dozen water striders
that love to conjure up the rain.
The gryphons dance, the dragons doze;
they all admire each other's clothes
while Sylvia teaches them to say
the spell she worked out yesterday
for turning pencils into pails
and failures into fairy tales.

About This Book

The cautionary tale about a powerful sorcerer and the servant who misuses his master's magic is drawn from a traditional fairy-tale motif that was popularized at the end of the eighteenth century by "Der Zauberlehrling," or "The Magician's Assistant," a poem by the German writer Johann Wolfgang von Goethe (1749–1832).

Goethe openly based his poem on a Greek dialogue translated as "The Lover of Lies," or "The Lie-Fancier," written in the second century by Lucian. In Lucian's tale, the companion of Pancrates, a holy man, observes his teacher's mysterious ability to speak a certain spell over the bar of a door, a broom, or even a pestle, making it take the appearance of a man who then goes off to perform the duties of a servant. After secretly overhearing the three-syllable spell of the holy man, the companion tries his hand at the spell on a pestle, telling it to carry water. Soon he discovers that he does not know how to make the pestle cease its actions; he then takes an ax and cuts the pestle in half, but now he has two water carriers instead of one, and the enchanted pestles fill the house with water until the holy man returns and transforms the pestle-servants into wood again.

Goethe's poem, in turn, presents a sorcerer's assistant who orders a battered broom to draw water from the river when the wizard's back is barely turned, only to find he lacks the means to reverse a rising flood. Again, the broom is chopped in half with an ax, and two water carriers extend the action into complete chaos.

The highly imaginative nature of the story and its universal appeal have attracted numerous writers, artists, musicians, and filmmakers over the years. In 1897, for example, the French composer Paul Dukas (1865–1935) created an orchestral work entitled *L'Apprenti sorcier*, or *The Sorcerer's Apprentice*, and this spirited musical interpretation of the story inspired American filmmaker Walt Disney (1901–1966) to choose it as the score for the well-known "Sorcerer's Apprentice" segment in *Fantasia*, his 1940 animated film.

In 1991, Newbery Medalist Nancy Willard and Caldecott Medalists Leo and Diane Dillon began their collaboration on a new version of the tale. In their creation of the sorcerer, Tottibo, his apprentice, Sylvia, and the fantastic creatures that inhabit their home, Willard and the Dillons have masterfully presented readers with a unique and utterly believable new world. Here is an unequalled feast for those who treasure and celebrate the human imagination — a book to pore over again and again.

0000108979634